Treasure Island

by Robert Louis Stevenson

#2 Off to Sea

Adapted by Catherine Nichols
Illustrated by Sally Wern Comport

Sterling Publishing Co., Inc.
New York

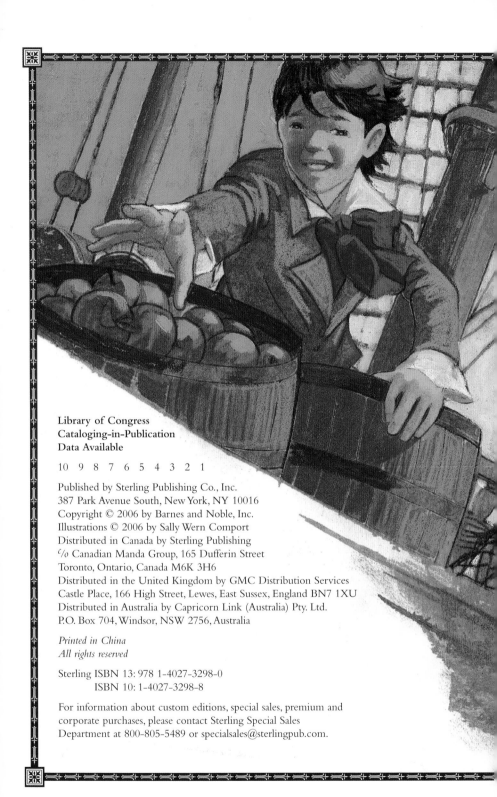

Library of Congress
Cataloging-in-Publication
Data Available

10 9 8 7 6 5 4 3 2 1

Published by Sterling Publishing Co., Inc.
387 Park Avenue South, New York, NY 10016
Copyright © 2006 by Barnes and Noble, Inc.
Illustrations © 2006 by Sally Wern Comport
Distributed in Canada by Sterling Publishing
C/o Canadian Manda Group, 165 Dufferin Street
Toronto, Ontario, Canada M6K 3H6
Distributed in the United Kingdom by GMC Distribution Services
Castle Place, 166 High Street, Lewes, East Sussex, England BN7 1XU
Distributed in Australia by Capricorn Link (Australia) Pty. Ltd.
P.O. Box 704, Windsor, NSW 2756, Australia

Sterling ISBN 13: 978 1-4027-3298-0
        ISBN 10: 1-4027-3298-8

For information about custom editions, special sales, premium and
corporate purchases, please contact Sterling Special Sales
Department at 800-805-5489 or specialsales@sterlingpub.com.

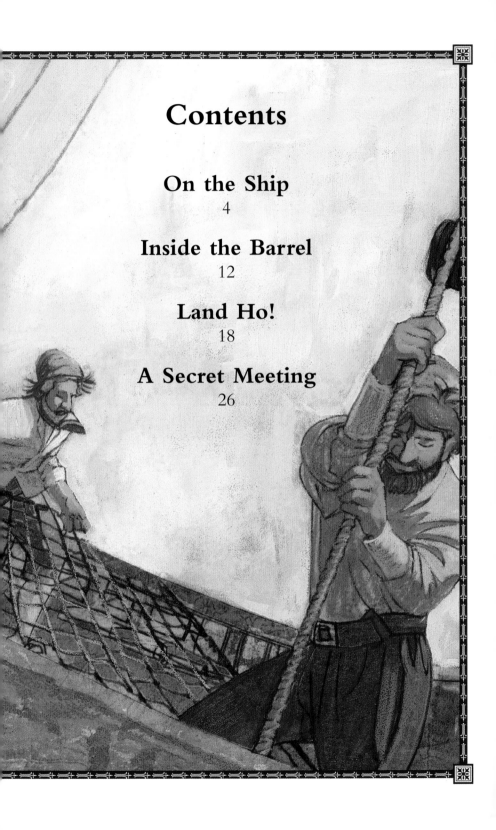

Contents

On the Ship

Jim Hawkins stood
on the ship's deck.
It was about to sail.
It was headed
for Treasure Island!
Pirates had buried
treasure there.
Jim and his friends
hoped to find it
and bring it back.

The anchor came out
of the deep, blue water.
Wind filled the sails.
"We're off!" cried Jim.

The ship's captain saw Jim.

"You, on deck," he said.

"Don't just stand there.

Go help the cook fix dinner."

Jim hurried away.

The cook's name was
Long John Silver.
Long John had a wooden leg.
He walked with a crutch.

"Come in, Jim," said Long John.

"Meet Captain Flint."

Jim looked around.

"Where is he?" Jim asked.

"I don't see anyone."

Long John pulled
a sheet off a cage.
Inside was a parrot.
"Hello! Hello!"
squawked the parrot.

"I named him after
a famous pirate,"
Long John said.
Jim let out a gasp.
Pirates scared him!

"Don't you worry,"
Long John said.
"There are no pirates
on this ship, Jim."
Jim felt much better.
Long John was his friend.
Jim could trust him.

Inside the Barrel

The days passed quickly.

Jim worked very hard.

The work made Jim hungry.

Luckily, there was plenty

of food on the ship.

There was even a whole

barrel of apples to pick from.

One day, Jim reached
into the barrel.
It was almost empty.
Just a few apples were
still at the bottom.
Jim climbed inside
to get one of them.

It was dark
inside the barrel.
Jim was tired.
He closed his eyes.
He would rest
for just a minute.

Jim dozed off.

Suddenly, he was jolted awake.

Someone was sitting next to the barrel.

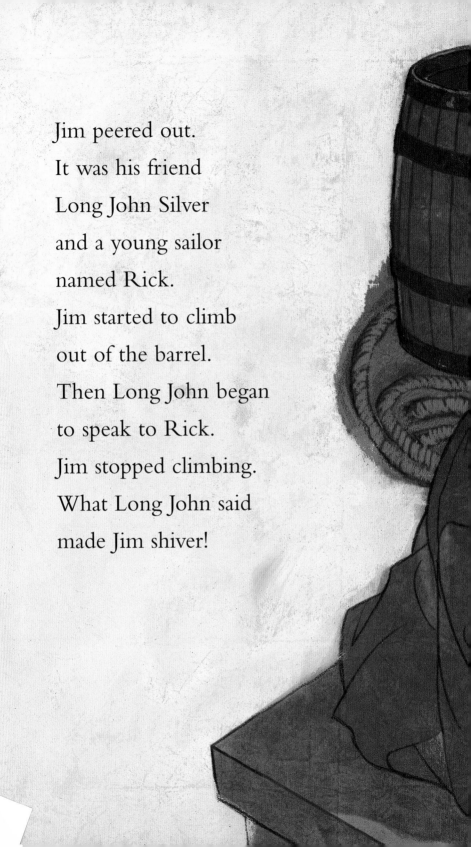

Jim peered out.
It was his friend
Long John Silver
and a young sailor
named Rick.
Jim started to climb
out of the barrel.
Then Long John began
to speak to Rick.
Jim stopped climbing.
What Long John said
made Jim shiver!

Land Ho!

"I sailed with Flint,"
Long John said.
"What a pirate he was!"
Inside the barrel,
Jim listened closely.
If Long John Silver
had sailed with Flint,
Long John was a pirate, too!

"I heard Flint buried
all his treasure," said Rick.

"Yes," Long John said.
"He buried it where
this ship is headed—
on Treasure Island!"

Then Long John told Rick
there were other pirates
right on this very ship!
Long John was their leader.
He asked Rick to join them.
Right away, Rick said, "Yes!"

"Good!" said Long John.
"When we get there,
we will let the captain
and his friends
find the treasure.
Then we will steal it!"

Jim was very angry.
Long John was not
his friend at all!
He was planning
to steal the treasure!

"All this treasure talk
has made me hungry,"
Long John told Rick.
"Bring me an apple."
Rick jumped to his feet.

Jim's heart pounded.
What would happen
if they found him?
Then Jim heard a shout—
"Land ho! Land ho!"

Land had been spotted!
After Long John and Rick
rushed to the deck
with the rest of the sailors,
Jim climbed out of the barrel.

A Secret Meeting

Jim joined the sailors.
In the distance was
Treasure Island!
Jim saw the captain.
Jim had to tell him
what he had heard.

The captain dropped his hat.
Jim picked it up.
"Here, sir," Jim said.
Then Jim whispered
that he needed to speak
with him in his cabin.
"Let's go, then,"
the captain said.

In the captain's cabin
were Jim's friends
Squire Trelawney
and Doctor Livesey.

"The boy here
has some news,"
said the captain.
"Speak up, then,"
the squire said.
So Jim told them
what he had heard.

When Jim finished,
there was silence.
Then the squire spoke.
"Pirates on my ship?"
We must get rid of them!"

"There are more of them
than of us," said the doctor.

"We must wait," said the captain.

"Wait?" the squire said.

"How will we know
what they are up to?"

Jim stepped forward.

"I could watch them," he said.

"I am only a boy, after all.

They will not suspect me.

I can tell you their plans.

Then you can take action."

The men agreed to the idea.

"Welcome to the team, Jim,"

said the squire.